# Classic MOVIE
## INSTRUMENTAL SOLOS

GW00673340

*Arranged by Bill Galliford, Ethan Neuburg and Tod Edmondson*

© 2010 Alfred Music
All Rights Reserved

**Alfred**

ISBN-10: 0-7390-7007-X
ISBN-13: 978-0-7390-7007-9

# Contents

# DING-DONG! THE WITCH IS DEAD

(from *The Wizard of Oz*)

Music by
HAROLD ARLEN

**Moderately bright march** (♩ = 116)

Ding-Dong! The Witch Is Dead - 5 - 1
35125

# CANTINA BAND

(from *Star Wars Episode IV: A New Hope*)

By
JOHN WILLIAMS

**Moderately fast ragtime** (♩ = 112)

Cantina Band - 4 - 1
35125

To Coda ⊕

# CONCERNING HOBBITS

(from *The Lord of the Rings: The Fellowship of the Ring*)

By
HOWARD SHORE

14

# JAMES BOND THEME

By
MONTY NORMAN

James Bond Theme - 4 - 1
35125

18

# GONNA FLY NOW

(Theme from *Rocky*)

By
BILL CONTI, AYN ROBBINS
and CAROL CONNORS

**Moderately** ♩ = 96

# RAIDERS MARCH

By
JOHN WILLIAMS

Raiders March - 4 - 1
35125

# FAMILY PORTRAIT

### (from *Harry Potter and the Sorcerer's Stone*)

By
JOHN WILLIAMS

25

*cresc. poco a poco*

*mf*

*rall.*

* An easier 8th-note alternative figure has been provided.

# HEDWIG'S THEME

(from *Harry Potter and the Sorcerer's Stone*)

By
JOHN WILLIAMS

**Misterioso** (♩ = 160)

Hedwig's Theme - 5 - 1
35125

A♯ = B♭.

# STAR WARS
## (Main Theme)

By
JOHN WILLIAMS

**Majestically, steady march (♩ = 108)**

Star Wars - 5 - 1
35125

Star Wars - 5 - 2
35125

# IN DREAMS

(from *The Lord of the Rings: The Fellowship of the Ring*)

Words and Music by
FRAN WALSH and
HOWARD SHORE

Moderately slow (♩ = 76)

(with pedal)

In Dreams - 3 - 1
35125

In Dreams - 3 - 3
35125

# SONG FROM M*A*S*H*
## (Suicide Is Painless)

Words and Music by
MIKE ALTMAN and JOHNNY MANDEL

Song from M*A*S*H* - 3 - 1
35125

*Enharmonic chord label (instead of A#13).

# OVER THE RAINBOW

(from *The Wizard of Oz*)

Music by
HAROLD ARLEN

**Slowly, with expression** ($\quarternote$ = 88)

(with pedal)

Over the Rainbow - 3 - 1
35125

50

# KEEP YOUR STUDENTS PLAYING WITH THESE GREAT PLAY-ALONGS

**Arranged for Flute, Clarinet, Alto Saxophone, Tenor Saxophone, Trumpet, Horn in F, Trombone, Piano Accompaniments, Violin*, Viola* and Cello*.**

*\* Piano Accompaniment included*

### LEVEL 1

**Easy Christmas Instrumental Solos**
Book & CD

**Easy Popular Movie Instrumental Solos**
Book & CD

**Easy Rock Instrumental Solos**
Book & CD

### LEVEL 2–3

**Classic Movie Instrumental Solos**
Book & CD

**Harry Potter™ Instrumental Solos**
(Movies 1–5)
Book & CD

**Indiana Jones and the Kingdom of the Crystal Skull Instrumental Solos**
Book & CD

**Lord of the Rings Instrumental Solos**
Book & CD

**Selections from Rolling Stone Magazine's 500 Greatest Songs of All Time: Instrumental Solos, Volumes 1 and 2**
Book & CD

**Star Wars® Instrumental Solos**
(Movies I–VI)
Book & CD

**Top Praise and Worship Instrumental Solos**
Book & CD

**The Wizard of Oz Instrumental Solos**
Book & CD

—— Visit **alfred.com** for more information ——

# INSTRUMENTAL ENSEMBLES FOR ALL SERIES

*Arr. Michael Story*

A versatile, fun series intended for like or mixed instruments to perform in any combination of instruments, regardless of skill level. All books are in score format with each line increasing in difficulty from grade 1 to grade 3–4. Perfect for concerts with family and friends, recitals, auditions, and festivals. Available for brass, woodwinds, strings, and percussion.

## Movie Duets for All

**Titles:** Double Trouble • In Dreams • Singin' in the Rain • The Entertainer • Twistin' the Night Away • We're Off to See the Wizard • Be Our Guest • Fame • Wonka's Welcome Song • Wizard Wheezes • Can You Read My Mind? • Star Wars • Everything I Do • I Don't Want to Miss a Thing • Living in America • Gonna Fly Now • Superman Theme.

## Movie Trios for All

**Titles:** Believe • As Time Goes By • Can't Fight the Moonlight • How the West Was Won (Main Title) • If I Only Had a Brain • Nimbus 2000 • You've Got a Friend in Me • Mamma Mia • Batman Theme • Cantina Band • Imperial March • James Bond Theme • Theme from Ice Castles (Through the Eyes of Love) • You're the One That I Want • Raiders March.

## Movie Quartets for All

**Titles:** Hedwig's Theme • Over the Rainbow • And All That Jazz • The Magnificent Seven • Theme from A Summer Place • Eye of the Tiger • There You'll Be • Blues in the Night • The Pink Panther • You're a Mean One, Mr. Grinch • Parade of Charioteers • Hakuna Matata.